I0659156

The Four Phases of Love

The Four Phases of Love

fRoM DeVeLopiNg lOvE to GRoWinG oLD

by: Daryl Horton

Abolitic Books, Twentynine Palms, California

Copyright © 2016 by Daryl Horton.

All rights reserved.

This book is a work of fiction. Names, characters, businesses, organizations, places, events and incidents either are the product of the author's imagination or are used fictitiously. Any resemblance to actual persons, living or dead, events, or locales is entirely coincidental.

No part of this book may be used or reproduced in any manner whatsoever without written permission except in the case of brief quotations embodied in critical articles or reviews.

Published by Poetic Abolition, an imprint of Abolitic Books, a division of Abolitic. For more information, contact the author and publisher at: poeticabolition@outlook.com or visit www.poeticabolition.com.

Cover, Photos, Art and Design by Daryl E. Horton

Printed in the United States of America.

Second Edition: April 2016

Library of Congress Control Number: 2016905286

PRINT: ISBN-10: 1-945047-01-1 | ISBN-13: 978-1-945047-01-5

MOBI: ISBN-10: 1-945047-04-6 | ISBN-13: 978-1-945047-04-6

EPUB: ISBN-10: 1-945047-05-4 | ISBN-13: 978-1-945047-05-3

The art and poetry contained in the pages of this book are dedicated to love –
coming in contact with it, bathing in it, striving for and against it, and learning
to understand it more and more with each passing day.

Contents at A Glance

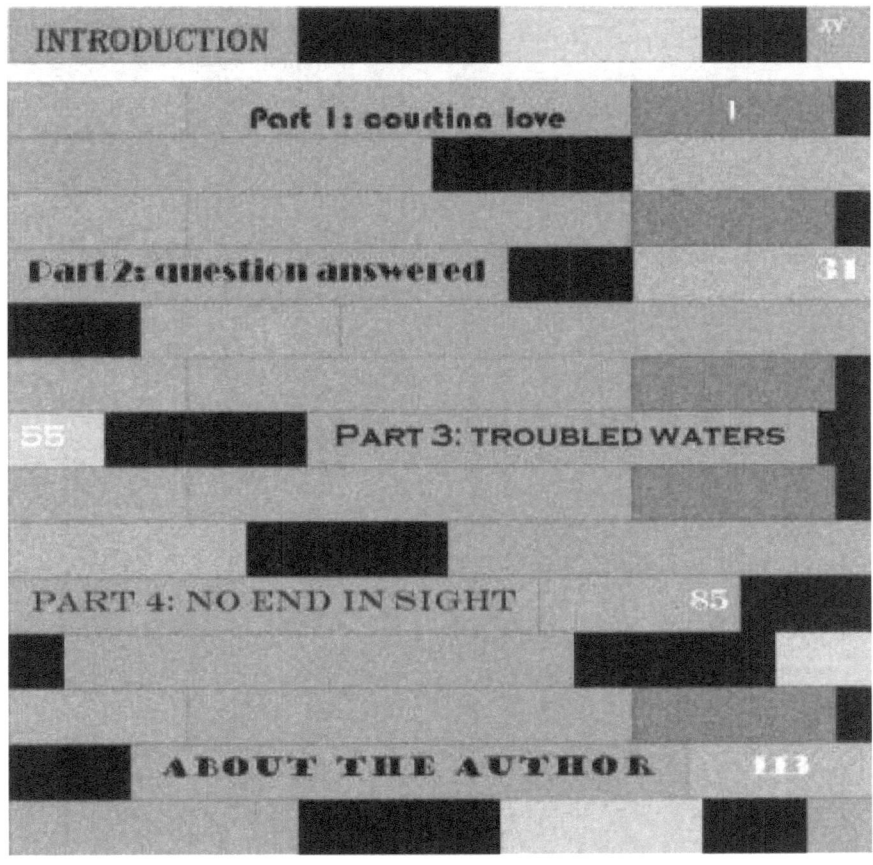

Table of Contents

List of Figures

Preface

Birth of an Idea

I began writing this book, because I was interested in publishing some of the poetry I've written over the years. I have many interests so finding the right theme was a bit of a challenge at first, but I finally decided to go with a general theme that many reflect on fairly often - Love. My goal was simple: select a few poems relevant to the theme that I could pull together in a short book. From there, my book began to take on a life of its own.

The book now had content, but it desired flesh. So what exactly does that mean? We all have a certain desire to acquire a specific look about ourselves and my book's desire was no different. So I began working out the details of how I could give this book the flesh it required. The answer was simple, I needed to give my book something people could gaze upon - art. But I had none readily available.

Like all new parents, I had encountered my first problem of parenting - how to satisfy the needs of my new born. I didn't have the time to create any art from scratch and I really didn't want to dive into the process of using someone else's art work. I did, however, have a few drawings I created many years ago.

As I sifted through my old drawings, I decided to look over pictures I had taken. Then it occurred to me that I could possibly use pictures instead of art. But, that changes the focus of my book and I had no interest in doing that. What I really needed was art, not photos.

I recalled that I actually had access to computer programs I could use to turn photos into works of art. I was elated and immediately went to work on drafting new works of art I could use to give my new born book the flesh it desired.

An Evolving Idea

I now had poetic content and artistic flesh. No longer a new born, my book had graduated to an adolescent. It was here I would be confronted with the next problem. My book now desired to become something important. We've all, at one time or another, questioned our existence, wondered what our real purpose was and searched for meaning. My book desired the same now.

It wasn't enough to talk about love and to look like someone. My book wanted to say something important about love. It wanted to establish some meaningful purpose to why it was engaged with the topic of love in the first place. From here I decided to add bits of advice and research to the works of art that accompanied the poetry. This small effort seemed to satisfy my book. It had a purpose now, which was to provide meaningful information about love to the reader. My book continued to mature at rapid rate.

Maturation

My book quickly entered the next phase of its existence - becoming an adult. As we grow older, having somewhat discovered what it is we want out of life, we move forward with what we believe is the right level of action required to bring it into existence. My book, no longer satisfied with simply having content, flesh, and meaning, now sought to make a difference. The work I had done so far taking care of my book led me to my next problem: what could I do to make a difference? This answer, was also simple - I could gather my book's content, flesh, and experience and erect a model other people could use to gain the same understanding of love I had gained.

Acknowledgments

The works in this book include poetry written over the last few years of my life. Putting this book together is a task I had been frequently putting off as I kept coming up with new excuses for why this was just not the right time. However, there are several people who urged and motivated me to take the time to write this book and so I'd like to thank my family – parents, siblings, and friends, for they have been the biggest inspirations in my life. I'd like to thank my wife who added to this book by appearing in the artistic photographs you'll see included. I would also like to thank God for blessing me with the talent and gift of creative writing.

Introduction

"The greatest lie ever told about love is that it sets you free." -Zadie Smith, On Beauty

"Wanna fly, you got to give up the shit that weighs you down." -Toni Morrison, Song of Solomon

The 4 Phases of Love

There are many models that describe the various phases of a loving relationship and I mention a few in the last part of this book. So how does my model of the phases of love differ? I offer a simple structure; a simple way of thinking about the phases one will encounter upon entering a relationship with another. The 4 phases of love include courtship, marriage, chaos, and utopia. Each phase is important to the maturing of a relationship. I won't, however, spend time dissecting each phase of this model in this book. Instead, I'll use the elements of storytelling to highlight some of various aspects of the 4 phase of love.

Fig. 1 *Model of the 4 Phases of Love* (2015).

The concepts concerning love, like religion, are fairly universal. What differs are the perspectives each unique individual will establish. We all believe in something greater than ourselves, but we also all have a different perspective and a way of defining what that means to us. Love and its phases are very much the same. I've provided the general concept and some context in the form of poetry, advice and research. It's up to you to decide what it means. I hope you enjoy the work contained in the pages of this book.

Part 1:

courting
love

Act 1: Plot Point 1

BLACK SCREEN

SUPER: THE COURTSHIP

FADE IN:

EXT. U.S.A. (2025).

Camera peers into complete darkness. An image of the United States begins to sharpen.

EXT. S.C. - DAY

Cars race through four lanes of highway in varying directions.

Screen goes black.

EXT. COLUMBIA S.C. - DAY

City sidewalks are filled with people walking in varying directions. Businessmen in suits carrying briefcases, women carrying babies, young teenagers running down the sidewalk, older people sitting on benches, and people exiting shops.

Screen goes black.

EXT. BOWLING ALLEY - DAY

The parking lot is filled with cars. Groups of people here and there having conversation.

INT. BOWLING ALLEY - DAY

The bowling alley is packed with people, young and old. Almost all bowling lanes are being used. Young kids huddle around the video arcade. Several people stand in line to order food, while others wait for drinks at the bar. People are sitting at tables eating, while others stand around in groups here and there, holding deep conversations in animated ways. Music is blaring and everyone seems to be really enjoying themselves. This is definitely the center of action for people living near the city.

AT THE BAR

TASHA, early thirties, curly black hair, short with an athletic build, stands alone, peering around the room while sipping from a glass of lemonade. She seems both a little annoyed and anxious, as if waiting for something to happen.

IN THE REST ROOM

MELIK, mid-thirties, low cut hair, medium height and athletic build leans over the sink to wash his hands. He looks defeated as he peers into mirror.

                    MELIK

        Well, looks like you failed to meet someone again
        buddy. Time to go home. Guess I'll grab a drink on the
        way out. Maybe that will cheer me up a bit.

AT THE BAR

Melik exists the rest room and walks toward the bar. He notices Tasha standing by herself and decides to say something to her.

4

MELIK

Hi, how you doing?

TASHA

I'm doing good.

MELIK

My name is Melik, what's yours?

She smiles.

TASHA

Tasha.

MELIK

Where are your friends?

TASHA

I'm not here with anyone.

MELIK

I ain't here with anyone either. There's an open table over there.
Care to sit together?

TASHA

That would be nice.

AT THE TABLE

Melik, much bolder and focused now, gets Tasha to open up more and they begin a conversation that lasts for hours.

CUT TO:

EXT. BOWLING ALLEY – NIGHT

Melik is seen entering the bowling alley. He seems to be looking earnestly for something or someone. He stops at the bar to ask if any of the employees have seen Tasha lately, but no one has seen her.

Melik and Tasha have been dating and seeing each other for several months, but now Melik seems to have suddenly lost contact with Tasha. He hasn't seen nor heard from her in several weeks. He's not sure what has happened, but he knows he doesn't want to lose her.

Melik spends the next few hours at the bar in a dark corner alone, thinking about Tasha and recalling the fun they've had up until now.

Confronting Desire

Truth is

Once eyes fell upon lips

curled into cheeks and

began tracing contours of

smooth ebony neck,

landing softly in

nest holding

two young fatten pigeons…

then s c a n n i n g

eyes captured the beauty of

legs running high, diving

into thick hips.

      Something happened to me man.

Heart skipped and puttered

legs stiffened as

pain like lightening flashed through left arm…

right hand, scrambling to wipe away

sweat from brow, left me

consumed in heat.

Legs finally gave out as body fell to floor

Eyes like video cameras

capturing the surprise in your face…

Eye could see the lips move but could (h)ear nothing at all.

As the bags in my chest deflated

White light engulfed my vision,

((shake))

Mind running in and out of consciousness

((shake))

Soft lips pressed firmly against mine

((shake))

Time itself refused to shift the clock another minute

((shake))

"Hey buddy, you ok?"

Broken from trance

Eyes quickly search the area but beauty has fled.

"Yes, I'll be ok once I

find the woman whose beauty stopped my heart."

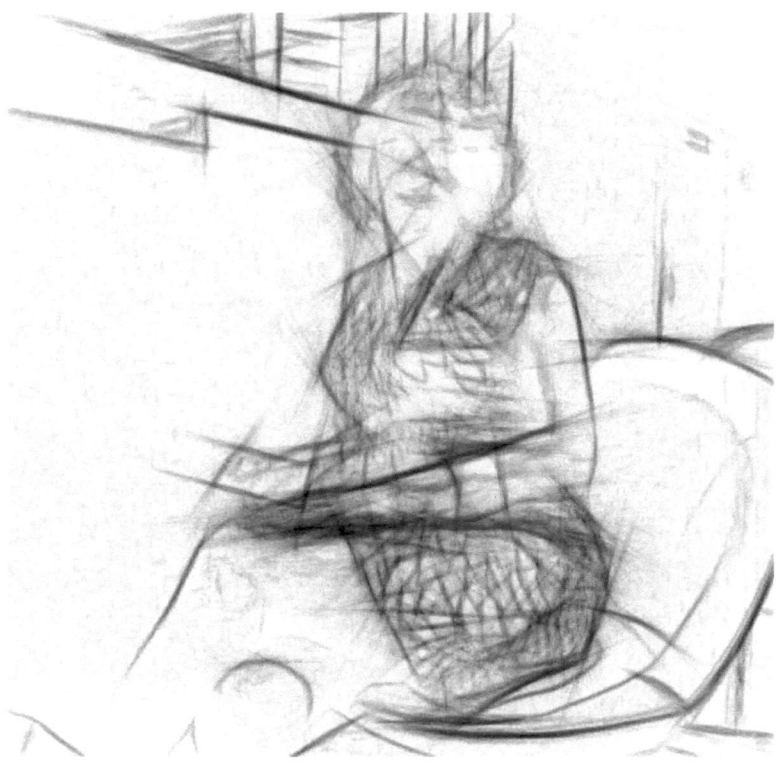

Fig. 2 *Imprint of Desire* (2015).

Desire, like many other sensations, is a type of feeling through which the transfer of specific information is relayed to our brains causing an action to be taken. Desire is described as a sense of want or need, which can be expressed through emotions and which can arise from various sources (Wikipedia, Desire). If we stop to consider that decision-making is an activity that falls along a spectrum moving from irrational to rational, you can understand the degree to which emotions can influence decision-making (Gutnik, Hakimzada and Yoskowitz).

A Deep Craving

My tongue could never tell a lie

For it publishes all that I feel,

My thoughts given life by my tongue

Can only illustrate what is real,

The passion that burns in my heart

Can be felt in the very words I speak,

I know no other way to express these emotions

Than to allow the air in my lungs to draw forth speech,

The fire inside cannot be quenched

Sensations to powerful to stop,

Continue to express love as only I know how

Until the love I seek is no longer sought,

      This love that grows will never lie,

      And the passion that burns will never die.

Incomplete Thought

Words

        Words

            Words

        Words never

Words never carried

        Words never carried more

Words never carried more meaning

than when careening, from your lips

I'm like a junky, fending, hoping

to secure a hit

veins protruding like power lines

awaiting a think prick

that sparks a surge

from which I emerge: changed

like the caterpillar from its crypt…

Chest Rhythms

Within this frame a heart beats fast

A presence invading my zone

       It was you I felt within my grasp

Within this frame a heart beats fast

With feelings like time are sure to last

       No longer must I walk alone

Within this frame a heart beats fast

       A presence invading my zone.

Nap of Neck

The back of her neck like

beautiful landscape of

clear valleys and

cool ponds.

Little hairs near the precipice of

her neck gently fold over like,

thin trees in blowing wind.

I'm lost in gaze, seeing my

lips kiss the

warm and smooth surface of

Love.

The breath of my nostrils restrained

by the beat of my heart, which beats

smoothly as lips prostrate

themselves on the surface of

warm brown skin. Sweet darkness

engulfs my sight as if I,

caught in a moment of prayer,

praying, for this moment to last forever.

Nap of Neck (Hakiu)

moist portions of flesh

embrace warm brown beauty of

smooth surface of neck.

Nap of Neck (Sonnet)

What is beauty, if not the neck of a woman

For I am often caught within gaze

The surface is like desert sands

Both smooth and plain and

Beyond the horizon exists an oasis of

Thin hairs that gently fall over as if

Trees and vegetation bending in the midst of

Breeze, from nostrils of man

Whose lips move with desirous intent

Connecting with the warm surface of love

     To see and not touch the beauty of her neck,

     Leaves me in gaze continuously vexed.

Nap of Neck (Triolet)

With these lips, in prayer, I prostate

Against the smooth surface of your neck

     Like sinful man fearful of my fate

With these lips, in prayer, I prostrate

Hoping to change the fortunes of my current state

     Like enslaved Hebrews constantly vexed

With these lips, in prayer, I prostrate

     Against the smooth surface of your neck.

Nap of Neck (Villanelle)

Your neck, by love, is more than flesh

Translating into material beyond the physical plain

My lips await love manifest

Love moves between worlds complex

Translating into material beyond a world of pain

Your neck, by love, is more than flesh

The language of love I yearn to confess

Translating into material beyond what's sane

My lips await love manifest

Words of love do more than caress

Translating into material beyond physical aim

Your neck, by love, is more than flesh

Through voice and tongue in love I bless

Translating into material beyond the physical name

My lips await love manifest

Love moves verbally beyond this text

Translating into material beyond the physical brain

Your neck, by love, is more than flesh

My lips await love manifest.

Nap of Neck (Sestina)

I gaze upon the beauty of your flesh

Filled with feelings existing complex

Lips move closer intending to confess

With passionate embrace and kiss of caress

Like monks with prayer in position to bless

With movements of love now made manifest.

Thoughts exceed the physical and become manifest

Taking on shape and form and flesh

Moving like the gods hoping to bless

With actions simple and yet complex

Using words, like fingers, I caress

Expressions of love I've been waiting to confess.

Actions speak louder than words I confess

Through simple motions a love manifest

Sound, like fingers on the small of back, caress

Slight squirms and jerks on plateaus of flesh

Thoughts foreplay on levels complex

On knees before alter, like priests, I bless.

My Egyptian priestess begs me to bless

A slave in heat I must confess

With Hebraic words of love, complex

Existing in everything and everywhere, manifest

Neither here nor there, spirit nor flesh

She awaits, silently, my verbal caress.

With words and sound and thought I caress

With nouns of spirit and soul, I bless

Through verbs we become twain flesh

Letters of blissful love I confess

Signed and sealed our thoughts manifest

Like syllables of poetry existing complex.

Emotions simplified no longer complex

Lips that burn with a passion to caress

With movement of thought from mind manifest

Like ancient men of wisdom ready to bless

We stand before God with praise I confess

The glorious beauty of creation in flesh.

With praise complex, like prophets who bless

With words caress, priestly lips confess

Love manifest, as lips press against flesh.

The Perfect Canvas

No pencil could trace the form I see before my eyes,

No paper could contain such a vision of loveliness,

I know no artist able to capture God's greatest creation,

No ink or paint can dispense her substance,

No canvas is worthy to hold her image,

No brush can speak her name,

There isn't a gallery that could embrace her form,

To even attempt to do so would spell shame.

Students study and research every line and curve,

Her very being is the foundation of artistic law,

She's the essence of love incarnate,

More beautiful than even the brightest star,

      There is nothing more beautiful than righteousness or wisdom,

      Except to have them both in women.

Fig. 3 *Sketched Beauty* (2015).

If ever there existed an agreement between art and science, it exists in beauty. The relationship that exists between art and science; between fiction and nonfiction; between subjectivity and objectivity, can be defined by beauty. Researchers recount examples of many in the world of science who experimented with art as a way of expressing the beauty in science (Girod).

This old heart of mine…

beats irregular patterns into

the canvas of my chest like

fists beating against the air

boxing shadows of

low self-esteem

"Just tell her how you feel fool,"

the voice in the back of my mind says as

speech struggles to get past clinched teeth

she looks in my direction and

stunned by the smile she threw my way

dizzy thoughts caused legs to wobble

step

        shuffle

step

        shuffle

the giggle her hands tried to hold back escaped

diving down openings buried in the sides of my head and

suddenly

i didn't feel so

....so

so nervous

       lips parched and fired back at her

Hi...it's very nice to meet you.

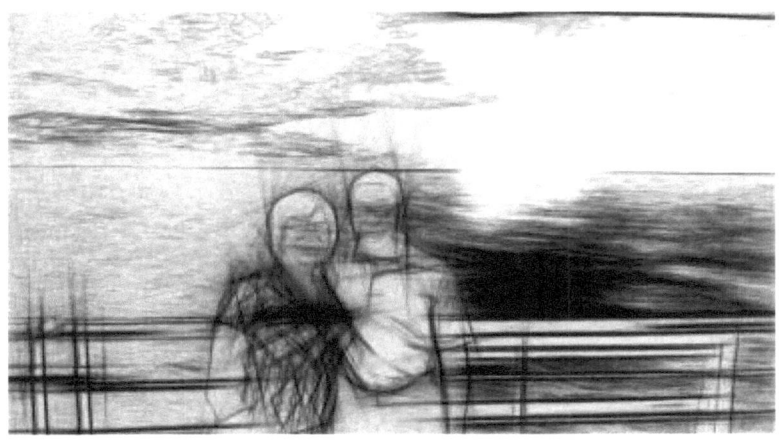

Fig. 4 *After Introductions* (2015).

The first introductions experienced by two people meeting for the first time is one of the most important moments in a relationship, but why? Relationships are extremely important, if not critical, to human beings and the survival of the human species (Larsen, Ommundsen and van der Veer). Many relationships often begin based on physical attractiveness, but the next most important factor in a lasting relationship is good conversation, which is one way of increasing intimacy. In fact, there are three factors which influence long relationships – intimacy, passion, and commitment (Larsen, Ommundsen and van der Veer) – and these three factors are known as the triangular theory of love (Wikipedia, Triangular theory of love).

Good conversation can improve the three factors that influence long relationships: intimacy, passion, and commitment. What you say and how you say it are important activities to understand, explore, and capitalize on after first introductions.

Wishful Dreaming

As dark as a moonless nights is my fair love,

Whose father plucked the stars from the sky,

She wears them now, dancing upon the feelings

Of my heart, with lovely voluptuous lips,

Beckoning and teasing with her sun-lite smile,

Long thick legs, jetty hair, a infectious glow,

A creature of un-imaginable beauty,

Encompassing the wildness of the wilderness,

Pure enchantment with each step,

I lose myself in her gaze, hoping, wishing,

Longing to embrace what I conceive to be a vision,

This young apparition, this beautiful mirage,

  A dream, could it all be a lie,

  If indeed a dream, may I never revive.

You and I Make We

(unfinished song lyrics)

She trying to say that we have time

But, time is running out

I give chase every minute, but

seconds don't amount

The clock just keeps on ticking

My days turn into nights

Mornings rush on by and

Our love has taken flight.

Fly away with me

Loose ourselves be free

Baby don't be alarmed

Find yourself in my arms

Because here…

you and I make we.

Fig. 5 *Good Together* (2015).

Another important aspect of a good relationship is knowing whether or not you are good for each other and if so, how do you maintain and even improve on those qualities that make you good for each other. There is no shortage of articles about this topic. Some articles provide checklists of items that can help you determine if you're good for each other. One such list includes thirty-one items that includes things you shouldn't do like hiding the relationship from others, to things you should do like inspiring each other to do better (Johnson). At the end of the day, however, if you keep the lines of communication open and if you remain flexible to the changes a relationship are sure to bring, you will be perfect for each other.

Plagiarized Love

Dear Love, please find forgiveness in your heart,

For I have plagiarized the beauty my eyes have seen,

I redraw you in my mind's eye when I am awake,

And again in my dreams when I lay asleep,

Fabricating copies with intentions to distribute

And hang them on the walls of my mind,

While enjoying life, I stole a look from you,

I am guilty and should be punished for this crime,

I tell myself that you belong to me,

And lock you away from prying eyes,

I am a prisoner, captivated by you, and

Not being near you makes the man in me want to cry,

>Will you pardon my crime and set my soul free,

>By taking the vow of a life forever with me?

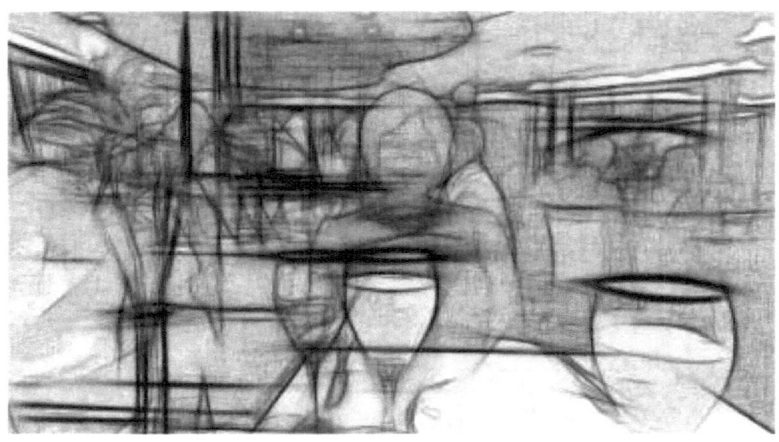

Fig. 6 *Recalling Love* (2015).

One of the strongest emotions we have aside from anger is love. Love has many manifestations and influences many of the actions we take. Love takes on different characteristics based on the culture from which it is expressed (Wikipedia, Love). One common perspective held by people around the world is that love represents what we value.

Part 2:

question
answered

Act 2: Plot Point 2

BLACK SCREEN

SUPER: GET THE GIRL

FADE IN:

EXT. THE MANOR - NIGHT

A few street lights scattered about provide insufficient lighting. It's a small neighborhood filled with apartment buildings and a few homes sprinkled here and there. All of the homes are close enough to one another to hear your neighbors snoring. The streets are littered with trash. A few dogs roam the area in packs, searching for food. Small groups of men occupy certain areas in the neighborhood as if they were providing security against anyone not a member of THE MANOR.

Melik has tracked Tasha to the Manor where she's staying with a relative. The Manor is one of the worse neighborhoods in Columbia. The people in this neighborhood are very territorial and getting Tasha out won't be easy. Even the police are afraid to enter this neighborhood. The fear Melik would normally have felt just thinking about entering the Manor has all but vanished. He seems to have gained strength and courage from his love for Tasha.

Tasha's relative lives in a home near the center of the Manor. There are three blocks of homes Melik must travel through before he reaches her.

EXT. DUMPSTER - CORNER OF 1ST BLOCK - NIGHT

Melik peers around the left side of the dumpster. Halfway down the street is a group of men, talking and smoking. Puffs of smoke encircle their heads. Melik can see a couple of men gripping hand guns.

MELIK

Crap. Guess I'm not going that way.

Melik peers around the right side of the dumpster. The adjacent street is clear, but getting down that street could mean exposing himself to the group of men on the left.

MELIK

Crap. Well, I could use the cover of darkness and the lack of street lights to conceal my movement. I just hope those guys are too focused on each other's conversation to notice me.

Melik moves slowly under the cover of darkness towards the adjacent street. As he approaches one of the homes, he just clears the view of the group of men when he notices a small KID on the porch staring at him.

EXT. ADJACENT STREET - NIGHT

KID

Hey.

MELIK

Hi little brother.

KID

Mommy, mommy, there's a shadow man in the yard!

Melik wasting no time, quickly moves past the house and the kid before the mother appears.

MELIK

That was close. I can't chance getting noticed by anyone here, especially since I don't live here.

Melik continues under the cover of darkness, evading another group of men with guns and a pack of dogs. It's not long before Melik reaches the home of Tasha's relative. He can see Tasha sitting on the front porch, crying. He quickly scans the area to see who else is out. He doesn't notice anyone else and moves toward Tasha.

EXT. HOME WHERE TASHA IS BEING HELD - NIGHT

MELIK

Tasha?

Tasha looks up, trying to find out who's calling her name.

MELIK

Tasha it's me, Melik.

Tasha rises and calls back to him.

TASHA

Melik!

Tasha quickly sits back down her cousin, DANNY, appears.

DANNY

Cuz, what's all that noise out here! Who you talking to?

TASHA

Nobody DANNY! Gone back inside.

DANNY

Whatever! I'm a turn the t.v. up and tune you out!

Melik made his way to the front porch and crouches beneath it.
He's so close he could reach out and snatch Danny from the porch
if he wanted to. Danny walks back inside. Melik and Tasha begin
whispering to each other.

MELIK

Tasha, I'm taking you back with me. Come on.

TASHA

Melik, I don't want to get you in any trouble. You better just go
back home.

MELIK

I ain't leaving without you. I ain't leaving without the woman I
love.

Tasha begins to cry again.

TASHA

I want to leave with you, but what about my family?

MELIK

If I have to, I'll deal with them, but for now let's just get out of
here. You see this hear ring. I want to marry you.

Melik clears his throat and drops to one knee.

MELIK

Tasha, from the moment we meant, I knew you were the one for me. I've never been happier than I have been over the last few months. Not being with you, is just downright painful. Will you marry me?

TASHA

Yes!

Tasha and Melik can hear footsteps in the house moving towards the front porch.

MELIK

Come on. Let's get out of here before your relatives try to stop us.

DANNY appears on the front porch just as Melik and Tasha escape. Melik and Tasha dart into the shadows of the night, following the same path out that Melik took to get in.

INT. BOWLING ALLEY - DAY

Melik and Tasha marry in the place they first met and begin a new life together far away from Columbia. They spend every day for the next several months, expressing their love for one another, riding the high of their new start together.

Beyond the Physical

Love is more than eyes can see

Eyes not blind to love manifest

Your eyes can see the love in me.

Windows of a soul made free

Birthed in love and covered in flesh

Love is more than eyes can see.

Hallways of a dying breed

Hands like lips that kiss and caress

Your eyes can see the love in me.

Corridors to a world of need

The beauty of your supple breast

Love is more than eyes can see.

We exist on levels now three

Like water we mingle our souls now blessed

Your eyes can see the love in me.

Music played on several keys

Becoming one in love no less

Love is more than eyes can see

Your eyes can see the love in me.

Contagion

Shortness of breath,

Colds chills and

sweaty skin,

I see the world before me as if

in a haze,

fighting to

Maintain consciousness but,

Thoughts seem to seek solace in the sounds of her voice.

You see,

Heart had been infected from

the moment our eyes met but,

seed had not taken root in mind so

time was needed before

lips could exchange

I dos.

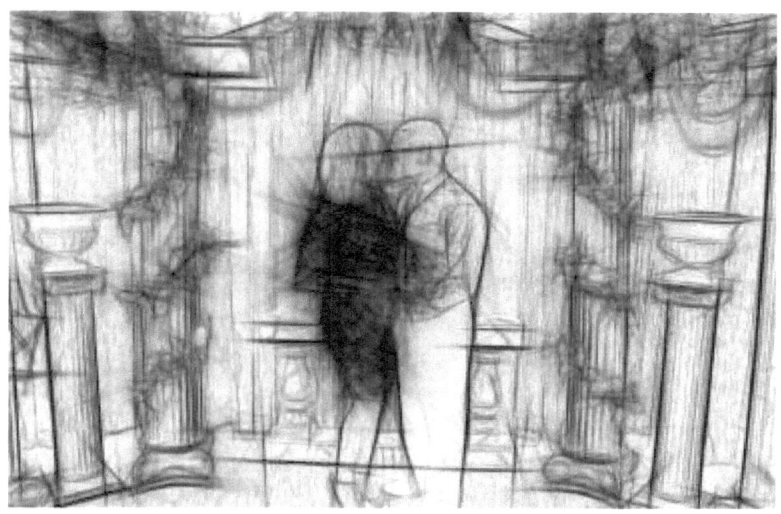

Fig. 7 *Exchanged Vows* (2015).

The idea of marriage vows originated with ancient human beings and in the case of Christian believers, it originated with the people of the Bible. Marriage vows were then referred to as a covenant. Marriage vows are simply formal and universal binding promises made by each partner on the day of marriage. The oldest marriage vows, in a traditional sense, were exchanged during the medieval period between the 5th to the 15th century (Wikipedia, Marriage vows).

The Love Trade

From the fairest creatures of this earth, I searched,

But I could find none comparable to you,

Whose love runs deep, like the rivers of the Nile

Who's more breathtaking than the morning dew

I sought the wise and searched the stars and could find no answer at all,

Even the spirits conjured by the soothsayer refused to hear my call,

It was night when at last I tossed and turned with visions not understood,

And by morning my heart burned with feelings, my tongue became its wood,

Like a flare in darkness, I finally realized, now everything was clear,

From balconies to rooftops, to pool pits, and in market squares,

I professed with such sincerity as could only be found in truth,

A love so incredible, as I had only found with you,

    What creature could hold such beauty for himself,

    Which cannot be contained by time, life, nor death?

Persistent Love

(sigh)...the world is

no less hazy than before and

her voice continues to

soothe the rhythms of my soul.

You see,

the infected heart and mind are intertwined

in the leaves of what grew from the seed

planted a year ago when we

like Babylonian gods and goddesses

imprisoned time and

abolished distance so

our love connection

would know no bounds...

there are no barriers, barricades, blockades or

any other boundaries capable of

casting a shadow on what we're building…

the strength of our love is buried deep inside

and as long as we hold tight

there's nothing we can't survive.

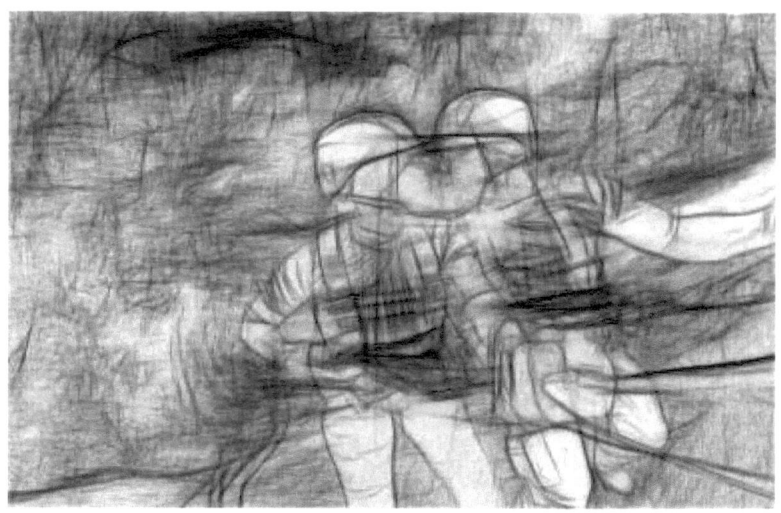

Fig. 8 *Adventurous Affection* (2015).

To have an affection for someone is to be in a state of being where one is influenced by an emotion or a feeling like that of endearment (Wikipedia, Affection). Since we have and express different kinds of emotions, we can also express different types of affection (Wikipedia, Affect (philosophy)) based on an emotion or even some combination of emotions, but the focus here is on bodily experience; a state of mind and body. I can both have affection for someone and be in an affect state of being; I can be in love and achieve a physical experience based on love. Since you can be in love and not experience love, you can view the state of being as being different from and not equal to the state of mind and body. One implies emotional contact while the other implies physical contact, but both are connected through the ability to generate a sensation. To have both would be pure bliss.

All I Need

All I want is your love

To share the bed

The soft silk sheets

To hold your warm brown body against my chest

Emotions of love

In times of sadness

To lay my head against your chest...

All I need is your love

When we're apart you fill my dreams

With anticipating thoughts of ecstacy

Love pure and bliss

Like calm oceans and cool breeze...

Give me your love

Tonight with slow enticing movements

Lets hold each other with a kiss

Slow exhales of deep heart felt passion

Tears of joy stream down our cheeks

Erected thoughts impel, pleased

With sharp movements and strong embrace

Twin moons perfectly round and voluptuous

Idle hands caress; massage

Biting lips with smiles of satisfaction...

All I want is your love

Give it to me.

One Heartbeat

((Booooom))

can ya fell da beat of ma heart,

beating, and beating, and beating, and

repeating da beating,

repeating, repeating, repeating

da beat of our heart,

love ma woman from da start,

paint a picture of our love and call it art,

never gone be apart,

escape tis world in the arms of our ark

cause

two twain in his name

garner his blessings from da start.

    2 People...

        1 Heartbeat...

Love.

Breath of life

From soft lips

Words like

Children dancing happily, traveled

Upon her breath

Carrening through atmosphere

Sound

Tapping the drum of my ear

Words…I listen

My eyes flutter

Air fills my lungs

And I became a living soul at hearing the words

"I love you."

Searching For Love

Within my bosom pounds a heart of love

Within this frame a soul enslaved by you

My all I would give at mere notice

Because this feeling I have is true.

Surely my thoughts have betrayed me

For I am dead to this world

Unless the love I seek, seek me in return

My soul shall be condemned a burning hell.

Whose kiss, like a saint, breeds life

Whose breathe is like the morning dew

Whose skin softer than the clouds of heaven

And as dark as the heavens in evening too.

      May my search end the misery of being single,

      And take me to the place where souls mingle.

Fig. 9 *House of Love* (2015).

How important is it to find someone you can love and be loved by? Human beings are social by nature – that is, they typically belong to groups of other like-minded people and others with similar inclinations. It is difficult for human beings to exist alone, although you can definitely find evidence of the contrary. Finding someone you can love and be loved by is part of the social programming embedded in our DNA. "Man is by nature a social animal; an individual who is unsocial naturally and not accidentally is either beneath our notice or more than human (Saunders)."

Give Me You

Give me you

I'll give you me

Let's become one.

My lips pressed against yours

Your lips pressed against mine

We breathe the same air.

My arms around your body

Your arms around my body

We share the same heat.

I touch, you feel

You touch, I feel

We are emotional.

Let me enter you

I'll let you take me in

We become one.

Beauty Undefined

I have known no shape as true as yours

Of which these eyes define,

No hips as wide nor lips as full

No other creation so divine.

No architect I've ever meant

Possessing skill so renown,

What tools used are able to perfect

Breasts and hips so round.

Not even the clearest lake found

Within the valleys of the day,

Sparkle like the light in your eyes

Whose origin only God can say.

     Your beauty is far beyond the price of jewels,

     Causing Cupids arrow to strike the heart of fools.

Fig. 10 *Eve: No Apple* (2015).

Eve and the apple story is one of the most well known stories from the Bible.
The story represents how man fell from a state of grace and into a state of
suffering and injustice. The story speaks to relationships and how influence
works in that it focuses on how Eve was first beguiled by a serpent,
representative of a deceiver, and then used to influence Adam, infecting him
with the same deception. The artwork above represents Eve in paradise,
surrounded by lush trees, but without the apple.

Part 3:

troubled

waters

Act 3: Climax

BLACK SCREEN

SUPER: LOOSING LOVE

FADE IN:

EXT. HOME - DAY

A two level house with a white picket fence and two cars in the driveway sits at the corner of LAKE and COVERTON. Yelling can be heard coming from inside of the home. A neighbor can be seen shaking his head as he waters his plants.

INT. HOME - DAY

Tasha, with her hands waving in the air, yells at Melik. Melik yells back as he turns to walk into the kitchen, leaving Tasha in the living room.

Melik and Tasha have been married for two years now. Their first year of marriage was everything they could hope for. They had escaped a danger and grew closer to each other as a result, but in their second year of marriage, things took a turn for the worse. Their communication with one another has become increasingly combative.

TASHA

I don't care if you don't think we need marriage counseling. We're going to get some!

MELIK

I never said we didn't need any counseling. You
definitely need all of the counseling you can get! In
fact, I'll set it up as soon as I can.

TASHA

What do you mean, I need all of the counseling I can
get? You're the one who seems to have a chip on his
shoulder all the time.

MELIK

Whatever. I'm not going to get into it with you again.
I'm calling someone I know to see if there's anyone
local we can see on short notice.

TASHA

Good!

Melik calls a friend about marriage counseling who puts him in touch with a
gentleman, DR JONES, in the area who specializes in young marriages. Melik
calls and sets up an appointment for the next day.

CUT TO:

INT. OFFICE OF DR JONES - DAY

Melik and Tasha enter the OFFICE OF DR JONES. The office is fairly large,
about the size of typically living room. Unlike other professionals, DR JONES
had no awards and certifications hung on the wall. There are only scenic works
of art, one hanging on each wall. He considers himself a very serious counselor
who views the "I love me" wall as a symbol of being more concerned with
oneself than with one's patients.

58

DR JONES had a large desk with a computer, books, and lots of paperwork atop it on one side of the room. A large 3-piece sofa set with a coffee table in the middle of the sofa, loveseat, and chair occupied the other side of the room.

DR JONES

Good morning, I'm DR JONES. Please have a seat on the sofa.

Melik and Tasha sit on opposite ends of the sofa. DR JONES continues talking.

DR JONES

First, let me welcome you and congratulate you on taking the first step necessary for strengthening your marriage. We'll handle the more administrative portion of this visit a little later. For now, let's get started. I already know why you're here, but I'd like to hear what you both think is actually going. Let's start with you Tasha.

TASHA

He's always mad at me about everything. It's like he doesn't think I can do anything right. He treats me like a child sometimes, calls me names other times, and rarely shows me any affection. When I ask him to do something, it's like petitioning the government for support. He expects too much and he never listens to me, I mean really listen to me.

DR JONES

Melik, your turn. What do you think is going on?

MELIK

She wants or needs everything done the way she wants it done when she wants it done. She spends money as if we have it growing on trees. She refuses to listen to reason. She fuses with me over petty things and takes every opportunity to accuse me of doing things I haven't done.

DR JONES

Ok, that's not a bad start for the two of you. I'm at least glad you have an idea of what some of the issues are you're dealing with. Now, tell me how does hearing what you each think is wrong make you feel?

INTECUT – TASHA/MELIK RESPONSES

TASHA

I do not spend money like it's growing on trees. I spend money on the things we need.

MELIK

I don't treat her like a child. If she doesn't know how to do something, I take the time to explain in detail how to do it so she understands and doesn't have to keep asking.

TASHA

I don't think this is going anywhere. Can we talk about the real problem? He doesn't treat me right.

                         MELIK

Oh, see. She's always got to be the focus of attention. I treat you better than you were treated before we met.

                         DR JONES

Please calm down. Let me guide this discussion and I promise you, you'll leave here happier than you arrived. But, this won't happen in one session. I'll need to see you both once a week.

                                                CUT TO:

INT. HOME - NIGHT

Tempers flare as Melik and Tasha argue and this argument seems to be the worse one yet. They go to sleep in separate rooms.

INT. HOME - MORNING

Melik awakens to find Tasha has packed a few bags and left, without even leaving a note. Visibly distraught, he considers what's been going on and begins questioning his marriage.

Confusions of Love

Against love, if ever love came,

Who am I to hold it guilty of neglect?

For my life, the only I've ever known

Without love, would be painful in retrospect,

For it is in the heart the desire of love burns

And it is in the flesh love is made manifest,

Though the quest for love is rarely fulfilled

The test of love, never simple, rather complex.

Fig. 11 *Chaotic Atmosphere* (2015).

Chaos represents disorder and confusion. At many points in our lives, we find ourselves in similar states of being. This is especially true in love relationships. The chaos that typically erupts in many relationships does so due to the lack of understanding that exists in relationships. The establishment of a relationship begins the real journey to understand one another. Relationships mark a very important change in the lives of two people. Real change...lasting change, typically, does not occur without the combination of both peaceful and violent action. There is an unbalancing that takes place after change occurs, but normalization - the re-balancing of life; the point at which the new replaces the old - is not far behind. Make no mistake about it, however, change does not occur without the falling away of the old state of being followed by the birth of the new state of being.

Gave Her My Heart

Gave her my heart

Was ready to

Give her my soul, but

Like leaves on their last limb

Fleeting feelings never seem to fall in the right place...

Is it true that

More can be said in silence than not?

I only wish

Space gave as much as silence does

Cause

Too much distance doesn't make the heart grow fond

Instead

Space, only adds more,

Space...

      (sigh)

There's a place where

The soul and spirit meet…

We

Were almost

There.

Have you ever felt like…

Pausing life

Frame by frame

So the feeling your heart pounded

Lasted forever?

You see she was more to me than just

Curves of winding beauty

Where the Sun chased Moon around the earth for days

More to me than just

Ocean caverns of feminine bliss

Where I felt as though I was trapped within a maze

More to me than just

Well, what I asked God for

A rib whose life I'd die to save

Frames…

Frames of

Separated images

Filled our storyboard with

Hours…

Spent between pillows and sheets

Deciphering body language

Students of Love studied

The montage of movements

Panning here, zooming there

In an attempt to capture passion:

Slow movements and

Skin glistening with beads of

Love Jones

Cameras caught images of

Light tug on hair

Hips rotating like lips

Swallowing manhood

As climax replicated over and over

We held each other tightly

Congealed in

What could only be interpreted as

Heaven, hoping

This moment continued

Without end.

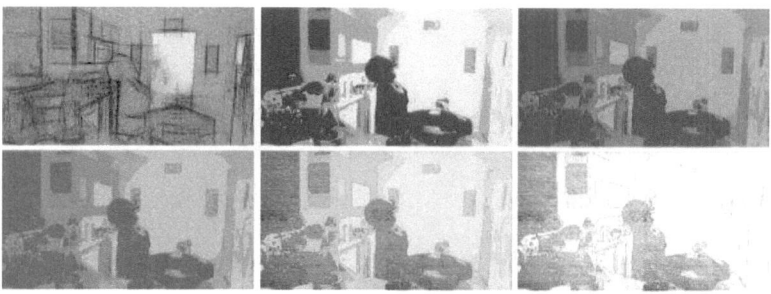

Fig. 12 *Framed Desire* (2015).

By now you are already acquainted with the concept of how desire can influence sensory perceptions, but let's take it a step further. Can desire actually influence the visual information your eyes receive? According to researchers, individual desires can cause desirable objects to appear closer than less desirable objects and this includes everything from food to stave off hunger to wining the lottery in order to escape poverty (Balcetis and Dunning).

Every time we open our eyes...every time we listen intently to the surrounding sounds, take in air and the various smells that occupy our nostrils, taste, touch, and feel things external to our bodies: we construct reality. Our individual truths are what form the foundation of our realities and truth is that which we can conceive and which we do perceive and agrees with the whole of our knowledge (Binet).

The connection between reality and desire is the influence of one on the other. What we desire most, becomes for us, reality. Make your love life a reality and bring the love of your life closer by strengthening your desire.

Heaven Sent

Memories of we

No longer exist,

Still when I think of you

And what we went through

I find it hard to reminisce,

I often walk

Alone on the beach

Tracing over our steps,

A feeling of love

When I held you tight

In my heart is what I felt,

I feel my sheets

Where we made love

Recalling every dent,

The heated passion

Late night sex

You were heaven sent.

Vacancy

Knew a girl once

we pranced upon the New Mexican plains

talked about hills where mountain men lived

exposed themselves once a year.

Knew a girl once who,

stole my heart but,

I was heartless

or, confused

unable to read the language of love.

Knew a girl once who

never gave up she,

had hope that love

could grow from a seed planted

so very long ago.

Knew a girl once

wish I knew her still

wish I, like the tin man,

could grow a heart...

could understand love...

maybe father time would

allow me to

turn back the hands of the clock.

missing you...

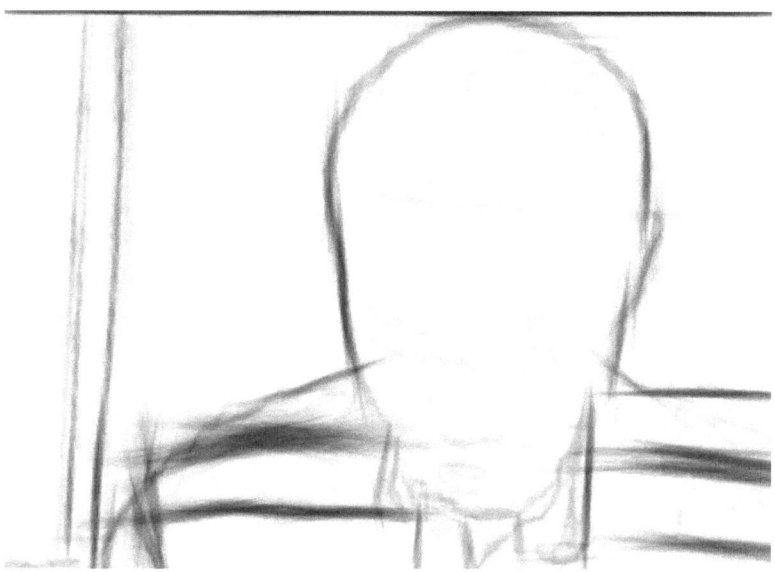

Fig. 13 *Regrettably Withdrawn* (2015).

As social beings, there is nothing worse than loosing someone you care about. Regardless of why the loss occurred, as social beings we crave the attention and affection of others. When we loose people we love, we go through periods of regret where we attempt to identify why the loss occurred. If we're not careful, we can end up blaming ourselves. Whether or not the individual is the cause of the loss is beside the point, since two people will always be required for interactions involving two people. Blaming ourselves can transform regret into disappointment and depression. Depression can result in the complete disruption of life that can be so extreme, it is literally considered an illness (NIH).

Missing You

An empty screen like an empty heart

I poured letters and sprinkled words on it

We conversed months...

A voice on the line, a chance to be felt

I dialed numbers endlessly stealing time to be alone

We spoke hours...

A screen once read like the gentle caress of fingers

A phone once used like the joining of two lips

I miss speaking with you.

Separated

I know not whether in this world or the last

Your beauty has been a part of my vision before

The innocence and compassion you hold for our people

Makes me want you more and more

Is it your smile I remember

Or the kink and the curl of your hair

The smell of your perfume skin

Or the empty feeling of once holding you near

My spirit won't let me rest, filled with

Memories of a time spent with you

My mind is compassed with feelings long past

Because in my heart, I know this is true

      Though rivers of time seek to keep us apart

      We remain inseparable through the bridge of our hearts

Fig. 14 *Made for Each Other* (2015).

Not to repeat myself, but if you keep the lines of communication open and if you remain flexible to the changes a relationship are sure to bring, you will be perfect for each other. For more discussion on the topic of being right for each other, refer to my comments on Fig. 5.

Emptiness

Like a man whose body seizes up

Arms grow stiff and useless

Legs unable to bear the weight fail to move

Thoughts become incoherent racing in

Different directions like wind

Lungs collapse like building under demolition

And heart struggles to pump life like

Frail new born struggling to grasp

Its first taste of oxygen and

Dry tears stain cheeks when I imagine

What falling out of love with you feels like.

Fig. 15 *Barren and Forgotten* (2015).

The other extreme of loosing someone is being forgotten and it can have the same effects resulting in the development of depression, if allowed to run its course.

Senseless Love

Sweetheart

I know it's been a while since

We last did not make love

And

I know it's been a while since

The last time I did not whisper

Sweet nothings in your ear

But you see

I didn't get lost in the rhythm of love

My heart didn't pound against my chest like

Bill collectors on the phone against eardrums

Instead of running towards a feeling I never felt before

My feet remained still like

      Like

            Like trees in midst of wind blowing in

      Many directions

From

Many directions

But

Never going anywhere.

Sweetheart

I know it's been a while since

The last time I never blew you a kiss

Or

The last time I never looked in your direction.

I know it's been a while since

The last time we never held hands

The last time lips never caressed one another

The last time I never thought about you

But you see

It wasn't until now

At this very moment

Seeing you in the arms of another man

That I felt so foolish for

Never taking a chance and

Saying never

Never again.

Looking Back

Use to look *forward*

toward a future together

sharing goals and ambitions

dreams with intentions like

newborns, maybe twins

from newlyweds to parenting grandkids

       instead

our heads swirled with thoughts

yearning for yester-years

because yesterday was not enough…

       feet seemed to carry us back

       two steps for every one

       we assumed carried us both

       in the same direction

…hinsight would have been

more welcomed as foresight and

maybe looking forward,

we would have seen

ourselves looking back.

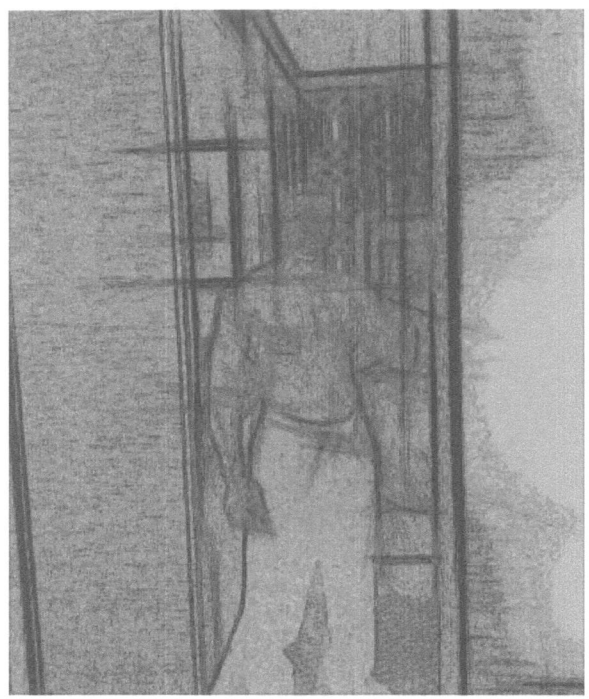

Fig. 16 *Mirrored Reflection* (2015).

Like a mirrored image, which looks back at you, we often find ourselves in states of deep reflection when things get difficult in our relationships. These moments of deep reflection can cause us to play the "what if" game. No the what if game is not some new couples game and this concept shouldn't conjure up images of people laughing and having fun. The what if game is a serious game where one contemplates whether or not getting involved was the right decision. From this first "what if" question, many more are generated. These questions only serve to hasten the demise of a relationship. Rather than play the "what if" game, spend time with your partner doing some root-cause-anlysis where you both participate in understanding what the problem is and how you might resolve it.

Part 4:

no end in sight

Act 3: Resolution

BLACK SCREEN

SUPER: RECLAIMING LOVE

FADE IN:

EXT. THE MANOR - DAY

Camera pans around then focuses on Melik.

It only took a few weeks of being alone again to convince Melik that he needed to find his wife and bring her home. He never thought he'd be standing in front of the Manor again. Love will have you do some crazy things and this was no exception.

Melik was tired of fighting with his wife. She still held the keys to his heart. Regardless of who's fault it was that they were having marital problems, Melik acknowledged that it was his responsibility as the man to ensure his wife's happiness. He had heard the phrase too many times. "Happy Wife, Happy Life." It now made sense to him.

All that has happened has brought him to this point; to this location again and this time, he didn't plan on ducking behind corners and hiding in the shadows. He'd walk right into the Manor, plead his case, and bring his wife home. Woe to anyone who stands in his way!

                                                            FADE OUT.

                            THE END

Boundless

Stone, nor iron, nor earth, nor endless sea

Mountains, ravines, nor principalities

Could keep me bound, imprisoned without cause

No jail, nor prison, nor iron bars

I move with haste, a yearning so plain

Only one with soft lips can douse this flame

Her eyes, her smile, connotations of love

I'd fight, I'd kill to protect my dove

Our love, for years, like a repeating song

Got me twisted, and lifted off these feelings now born

Low whispers, deep love, satisfaction guaranteed

Many kisses, plenty sex, bringing forth my seed

     What earth, what world could do us any harm

     Nothing and I'm convinced we'll die in each others arms.

Laugh with You

I wanna laugh with you…

I wanna shoot the shit!

and veg out, when

There ain't nothing more important than us.

Life is short and

The world ain't really that big so,

Let's get lost in each other

As often

As

We

Can….

Nothing else really matters.

Fig. 17 *Blissful Love* (2015).

The relationship journey two individuals embark on passes through several phases. There are varying perspectives on the number of phases a typical relationship will go through. The 3 phased relationship includes the intoxication stage, the flashback stage, and the co-creativity stage (McGee and Taylor). The 5 phased relationship model includes the romance stage, the power struggle stage, the stability stage, the commitment stage, and the co-creation or bliss stage (Muzik). One other model lists 9 phases which includes the infatuation stage, the understanding stage, the stage of disturbances, the opinion maker stage, the molding stage, the happy stage, the stage of doubts, the sexual exploration stage, and the stage of complete trust (Arthur). Regardless of the number of stages that exist or what you call them, the final stage is one in which you will enjoy perfect happiness and is marked by your truly becoming one.

Interchanges of Love

Words leap from lips

Separating into

Vowels and consonants

Careening ever closer to caverns where

Drums placed in ears eagerly await every

Syllable transferred through the medium of

Space...

Frontal lobe

Like small computers,

Reassembling packets of

Nouns and verbs

Into statements that,

Color the canvas of heart,

Painting images that

Can only be captured by

Expressions shared between

Two

In

Love…

You see

Cupid makes daily visits

With each conversation

I share

With my

Valentine.

Nine Months Later

Eyes open and

First breath taken in a world foreign

Although hands now small memories preserve

a life prior with one heart aches to find again

...fast forward...moving past

days

    weeks

        years

Gone by and yet

A feeling of disconnection seems to pervade like

Rib missing from chest

Then, by chance...is it really you...before this life

You and I...and now...husband and wife...again

....Always & Forever....

Fig. 18 *Irreplaceable Love* (2015).

My wife likes to remind me of just how much I should value her, often stating that I'd never find another like her. There is a lot of truth to this statement. Beside the fact that we are all uniquely different from one another, we spend a lot of time and effort learning from one another, gaining a better understanding of each other, and really merging our personalities. Companies who have to say goodbye to employees who've been with the company for many years know all to well just how difficult it is to replace long-term employees. This irreplaceable aspect of the long-term employee is also true for long-term partners in a relationship. You literally will not find another one quite like your partner.

Sensually Eager

The hum of lips

pressed against

the side of her neck like

The strum of the viola as he

Bellows beautiful base-filled sounds

That describe

yearnings of man returning from

year

spent in

war

away from

Soft lips and perfumed skin

Spent days in self-education program

He studied the art of extended foreplay

Graduated with masters in kama sutra

Promised to cover every inch of her in

The sounds of love

Bodies already glistening with hours of gratification

Heat from passion and smoke from incense

Filled the low-lite room with

Atmosphere of ecstasy explorations as

Passion gave way to immortality.

Beyond Sight

How can I love you with these eyes alone

When your beauty is more than I can bare,

My mind has devised ways to love beyond sight

Constantly thinking of physical means are things I shouldn't dare,

Perhaps I can taste with these lips what the eyes have seen,

Even a touch would convince me this wasn't a dream,

The passion in me burns with each thought of you, filled with

Fantasies of things I hope are more than what they seem,

Your smell, like the fragrance of roses, encircles me as

My thoughts, no longer under my control, compel me to move,

My tongue eager to speak words able to capture every feeling I have

Describing emotions I'm sure I can more than prove,

　　　For if love could be contained in these eyes alone,

　　　There would never be a reason to ever leave home.

Incalculable

If you love me, then love me without fail.

For in return, I will love you without end.

Never before have I wanted someone more,

For in this game of love, do whatever it takes to win.

If you kiss me, then let the kiss last for hours.

Yea let the embrace of our lips last for years,

For these lips burn with a thirst unquenchable

And not tasting your lips is my only fear.

If you touch me, then let it be as the hand of an angel,

For in this will I feel blessed.

Let us hold one another and never let go,

For with your love am I obsessed.

> Let us two become as one inseparable,
>
> Whose love, like an ocean, is immeasurable.

Fig. 19 *Wayfaring Love* (2015).

For relationships to grow, some action is required. I like to refer to this action requirement as the wayfaring aspect of love. It wasn't until I left home that I began to understand that the world was a much bigger place than where I had grown up until then. Something happens when you travel to places distant from where you grew up. You begin to grow as you learn about the other areas of life and of the world. These experiences, as you continue to develop them, are what form the structure of your wisdom. Relationships need this experience building aspect of life as well. As mentioned previously in my notes about affection in Fig. 8, there are three types: state of being, state of mind and state of body. The wayfarer will need all three in the quest to achieve a long-term relationship. The final phases of a long-term relationship require something more than simply physical contact, it requires experiential contact so travel often and spend time developing rich experiences together.

One Plus One Equals One

Flung into contortions through infliction of heart's disease

Symptoms: overbearing fear, sweaty palms, weak knees

Heart races against sanity playing catch up games to retreating mind

Lungs struggle to inflate as soul's windows strain to peer beyond the blinds

Sight has failed to do as it has done in the past – guide feet

Instead, regressed from brilliant tactician to babbling fool of the street.

Have I become humanity's jest?

My life, another chapter in the book of satire?

The loneliness of darkness surrounds me but

I seek

A glimpse of the light of companionship and

Try as I might, I fight as any boy would for girl

Trying senselessly to make sense of senselessness in a senseless world.

Like wildfires, heart's disease spreads uncontrollably to thought regions

Brain barriers built to block heart's blasphemy bend under the weight of heart's legions

And mind wonders…

Visions of happiness and joy have me wondering if this is what death feels like or is this just life? Am I to live infected with this virus making me L-O-V-E positive. Will you accept me with all my faults and issues? Can you deal with all the goodbyes and miss-you-s? Will you still love me when times are good and bad, and happy or sad? Of course, making up will be so sweet, making love between the sheets, the long kisses and slow caress, the way the sweat beads up upon your breast, your dark and beautiful flesh as our love begins to mesh, your serious smile lets me know this is more than just fun as one plus one becomes one.

Insanity's vice grips as feet move in direction eyes can't see

Guided by the warmth felt skin deep

Hands grope blankets of darkness reaching for light's sheets

Hoping heart finds what mind seems content in refusing to seek

But the knot in throat pausing lip's speech reveals fields of

E m o t i o n

And

Having discovered entrance to love, hands fall to side as feet stop and

Releases empty weakness like buckets of water from the river of self

Thought clears, lips part, and three words leap from the tongue of boy

Hitting girl in face:

I Love You.

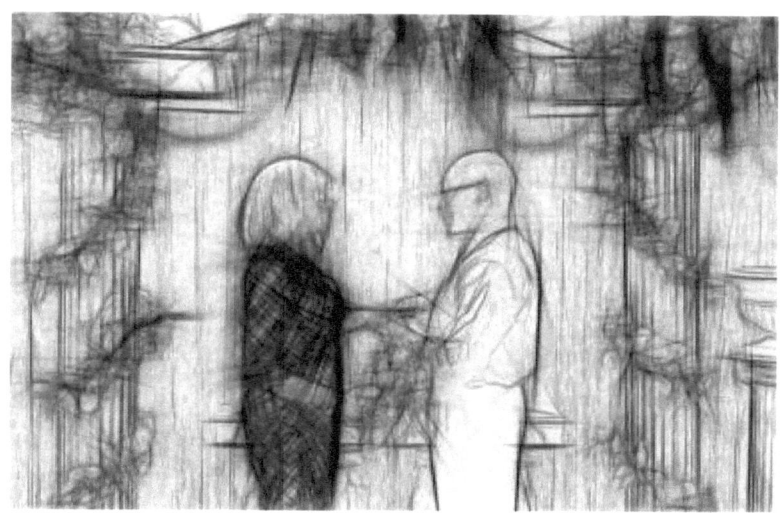

Fig. 20 *Indissoluble Vows* (2015).

We've all spoken to someone whose been married to the same person for more than thirty years. We've even seen pictures of couples who've lasted well into the triple digits in age. These type of relationships don't have to just be the stuff love stories are made of. These stories can be our reality. Take some time to identify ways to strengthen the bond between you and your partner.

Until the day we...

close our eyes

never to open them again

by the oath we took

and never shall break

our love shall remain until the end.

Infinite Adoration

"There is no end of all the people, even of all that have been before them..."
(King James Version Compact Reference Bible, Ecc. 4.16)

"The small and the great are there...which rejoice exceedingly, and are glad,
when they can find the grave?" (King James Version Compact Reference
Bible, Job 3)

Age has its limit

and the flesh must eventually fail

but the spirit is everlasting

and my love for you shall prevail

when the end has come and

our breath has ceased

in death, as Job described

is where we will all sleep

we shall rest for a time

until we are born again

remembering nothing of what has gone before

our lives cycle without end

so until we meet once more

in a life soon renewed

i promise to love infinitely

the woman to whom i am glued.

Fig. 21 *Timeless Love* (2015).

Some believe Solomon spoke of reincarnation as he discusses various cycles that exist in nature and in the same breathe, stating that there will be no end to all people, yet there is a finite number of people who will ever exist. Many believe this suggests that all who have been will be again (Zondervan). Whether this is true or not, I'd like to think that I'll get the opportunity to live another lifetime with the woman of my heart.

Bibliography

Arthur, Elizabeth. *9 Relationship Stages That All Couples Go Through*. 28
    December 2015. Web. 28 December 2015.
    <http://www.lovepanky.com/love-couch/romantic-love/relationship-
    stages>.

Balcetis, Emily and David Dunning. "Wishful seeing more desired objects are
    seen as closer." *Psychological science* (2009): 21(1) 147-152 .
    Document.

Binet, Alfred. *The Mind and the Brain*. Cambridge: Paul, Trench, Trübner &
    Company, 1907. Book.

Girod, Mark. "A conceptual overview of the role of beauty and aesthetics in
    science and science education." 6 March 2006. *Western Oregon
    University*. Document. 28 December 2015.
    <https://www.wou.edu/~girodm/litreview.pdf>.

Gutnik, L. A., et al. "The role of emotion in decision-making: A cognitive
    neuroeconomic approach towards understanding sexual risk behavior."
    Journal of biomedical informatics 39(6) (2006): 720-736. Document.

Johnson, Margaret. *31 Ways To Know You're In The Right Relationship*. 19 June
    2012. Webpage. 28 December 2015.
    <http://www.huffingtonpost.com/2012/06/19/31-ways-to-know-youre-
    in-the-right-relationship-advice_n_1608813.html>.

Larsen, Knud S., Reidar Ommundsen and Kees van der Veer. *Rozeberg
    Quarterly*. 28 December 2008. Web. 28 December 2015.

<http://rozenbergquarterly.com/attraction-and-relationships-the-journey-from-initial-attachments-to-romantic-love/>.

McGee, Seana and Maurice Taylor. *The 3 Phases of Every Relationship*. 1 September 2012. Web. 28 December 2015. <http://spiritualityhealth.com/articles/3-phases-every-relationship>.

Muzik, Bruce. *Why do some relationships break up and others last a lifetime?* 28 December 2015. Web. 28 December 2015. <http://www.loveatfirstfight.com/relationship-advice/relationship-stages/>.

NIH. *Depression*. 28 December 2015. Web. 28 December 2015. <https://www.nimh.nih.gov/health/topics/depression/index.shtml>.

Saunders, Trevor J. *Aristotle: Politics: books I and II*. Oxford: Clarendon Press, 1995. Book.

Wikipedia. *Affect (philosophy)* . 14 December 2015. Web. 31 December 2015.

—. *Affection*. 14 October 2015. Web. 28 December 2015. <https://en.wikipedia.org/w/index.php?title=Affection&oldid=685715338>.

—. *Desire*. Vers. 695319552. 15 December 2015. Web. 28 December 2015. <https://en.wikipedia.org/w/index.php?title=Desire&oldid=695319552>.

—. *Love*. 23 December 2015. Web. 28 December 2015. <https://en.wikipedia.org/w/index.php?title=Love&oldid=696532230>.

—. *Marriage vows*. 16 November 2015. Web. 28 December 2015. <https://en.wikipedia.org/w/index.php?title=Marriage_vows&oldid=690891918>.

—. *Triangular theory of love*. 13 December 2015. Web. 28 December 2015.
      <https://en.wikipedia.org/w/index.php?title=Triangular_theory_of_love
      &oldid=695109132>.

Zondervan. "Ecclesiastes." Solomon. *King James Version Compact Reference
      Bible*. Grand Rapids: Zondervan, 1611. Ecc. 4.16. Book.

About the Author

Daryl Horton was born in 1976 in Detroit MI but grew up in Hopkins and Columbia SC. After graduating from the U.S. Naval Academy in 2000 with a B.S. in English, Daryl joined the U.S. Marine Corps and spent the next 11 years serving his country.

Daryl currently works as an information and knowledge manager specializing in creating and sustaining learning organizations in chaotic and often complex environments. His educational background includes an MFA in Creative Writing from National University and an a Masters in Information Systems Management specializing in business information management from Walden University.

Daryl has written for and participated in several writing forums, contests, and magazines where he sometimes writes under the pen names Subconscious and The Abolitionist. Some of the themes Daryl's work revolves around include spirituality, love, history, activism and philosophy.

If you've enjoyed reading this book, please leave a comment on the Amazon page for this book. Thank you.

Contact Daryl at poeticabolition@outlook.com or, to find out more, visit www.poeticabolition.com

Other Books by the Author

This is a young adult drama about young husband in his mid-twenties who joins the military hoping to make a better living for his family and ends up getting deployed during his first year as a Marine.

He's a deeply religious man who believes his marriage is doing great, but everyone else who knows him and his wife seems to see things differently.

Deploying to combat not only changes him, but it opens his eyes to what's really going on in his marriage. As much as he wants to save his marriage, he has to contend with the impact that being deployed will not only have on him, but also his wife and their marriage.

This is a story that highlights an area of military life that is often overlooked by media and by the many organizations that provide support to military members, veterans, and their families. I hope you find this book both creatively interesting and informative.

Pickup this your pring copy of Deployed: A State of Human Conflict at Amazon (http://amzn.to/1qz66ZW). Pickup the digital version of Deployed: A State of Human Conflict at fine ebook retailers everywhere.

Poetic  Abolition

www.ingramcontent.com/pod-product-compliance
Lightning Source LLC
Chambersburg PA
CBHW050800250626
47155CB00005B/2154